The Footballer from Outer Space

Books For Boys

IAN WHYBROW

ILLUSTRATED BY MARK BEECH

Hodder Children's

For my good neighbour, Thomas Campbell,
noted entrepreneur, originator of the plum-run
and inventor of all sorts of remarkable
wheezes and devices, with grateful thanks.

Text copyright © 2014 Ian Whybrow
Illustrations copyright © 2014 Mark Beech
First published in Great Britain in 2014
by Hodder Children's Books

2

A Catalogue record for this book is available from the British Library

ISBN 978 1 444 91576 1

Printed and bound in Great Britain by CPI Group (UK) Ltd, Croydon, CR0 4YY

The paper and board used in this paperback by
Hodder Children's Books are natural recyclable products made from
wood grown in sustainable forests. The manufacturing processes conform
to the environmental regulations of the country of origin.

Hodder Children's Books
A division of Hachette Children's Books
338 Euston Road, London NW1 3BH
An Hachette UK company
www.hachette.co.uk

Crash!

Ker-poom!

That was the main thing in Tom Campbell's head that afternoon as he zoomed along the narrow lane to Hopley's Green and approached the blind corner ... Ker-poom! Ker-poom!

He was standing on the pedals of his beaten-up BMX, late for a kick-about with some mates on Spearmarsh Common. Last time he'd played, he'd been rubbish and Peter had said so. He hadn't put a single shot past Logie in goal.

"This time it's going to be different – Ker-poom!" he said through gritted teeth.

That morning his mum had told him off for wasting his time playing with rowdies like Ned and Kyle and Peter. Why couldn't he make friends with nice quiet boys? And when he'd answered back, she'd sent him down the orchard to pick more plums for jam.

He'd been there a good while

before he started nailing together long bits of wood to complete his latest invention: a plum-run, a cross between a gutter and a helter-skelter with sharp angles at the elbows. The plums wobbled comically down, jerkily but gently, and they settled un-bruised into handy heaps.

Now he was late for the game. His mates would think he'd chickened out – which was why he was pedalling along as fast as he could.

Hedges grew tall on each side of the lane. The idea of the hedges was to keep sheep in the fields and off the road. But the thing about sheep is, they spend a lot of time looking for gaps underneath hedges that are big enough to squeeze through.

Tom knew this, being a country lad, but he bombed onwards anyway. Ker-poom! Ker-poom!

His whole body was shaking with the effort of holding on to his handlebars while gripping the football under one arm. Suddenly, a sheep shot out of the hedge like a huge lump of soap from a wet fist and tried to barge Tom into a muddy ditch.

Tom was startled but his reflexes were excellent. He shifted his weight, left the road, and skimmed up along the grassy bank under the hedgerow like a stunt-rider on the Wall of Death.

"Baaa ... aa ... aa," muttered the sheep.

Ah, if only. If only Tom hadn't

turned to shout, "Ha ha! You missed me, mutton-brain!" But he did. And just for a second he took his eye off what was in front of him.

Perhaps these things are written in the stars. Anyway, he saw too late that he was speeding straight towards the sturdy trunk of an ash tree. The only way to miss it was to crash

into a silver spacecraft that lay still
and stranded right beside it on the
very edge of Hopley's Green.

KER-POOM!

The Visitor

As it turned out, it was the bike and the football that hit the tree-trunk and Tom who crashed into the spacecraft.

Not that Tom realised it was a spacecraft. As a matter of fact, he thought it was some sort of shiny aluminium motor-home. Still, it was a good thing that it was a spacecraft, because otherwise he might have broken his neck.

Luckily the spacecraft was made of a friction-reducing material, so it was just as if Tom had dived into a caravan-sized marshmallow. He was entirely unhurt but that didn't stop him making rather a fuss – hopping about, feeling himself for dents and lumps, and going, "OOOCH! YOWCH! OOOCH!"

It always took Tom a bit of time to make a fuss, so he didn't notice straight away the pair of boots that stuck out from under the motor-home, or whatever it was. If he hadn't been so upset about his bike he might have gone to take a closer look. But his bike was a twisted wreck and he shouted, "Oh no! Dad's gonna KILL me!"

"Hey! Give over!" came an anxious, muffled voice. "No killin'!"

"What?" yelled Tom, spinning around. That was when he finally noticed the boots. They were unlike any other boots he had ever seen. They shone like glass and changed colour every few seconds.

"I come in peace!" said the voice again. "I'm tryin' to fix something!"

"What?" repeated Tom. He felt nervous because he knew that voice – yet it was still odd. It was all on one note, somehow; like a computer-voice. A moment later the owner of the voice crawled out into the sunshine and scrambled to his feet.

Tom's mouth dropped open and his eyes nearly pinged out of his head. There in front of him stood a boy-sized version of his hero, Wayne Rooney. He looked exactly like Wayne Rooney looked on telly, only he was Tom's size. He was standing with his hands up. And he was bright blue. Tom didn't move. He couldn't. His mind raced as he tried to make sense of the kid he was looking at.

"Y-you're Wayne Rooney, aren't you?" Tom asked at last, feeling stupid. After all, the kid looked exactly like Wayne Rooney, except that the parts of his body that were showing, including his round face with the scar under the bottom lip, his powerful neck and muscular arms, were the colour of the sky. And he had weird eyes. They seemed to revolve like miniature misty blue planets.

When there was no answer, Tom added, "I've got a football somewhere. You wouldn't fancy a kick-about, would you?"

"Yeah, call me Wayne," said the kid. "Or Visitor."

"Visitor?"

"Yeah. Where I come from, I don't use a name, see. We're all called the same there. Beep. When we want to send a message, we use the Thought-Way."

At that moment, everything emptied out of Tom's head like water down a plughole – the crash, the possibility of bumps and bruises – everything except a warning: "This is too weird! Run for your life!"

Yet the blue boy trembling in front of him didn't look dangerous. If anything, he looked nervous and upset. It occurred to Tom that he might also be hurt. "Are you all right, mate?" he enquired hesitantly. "Sorry. I couldn't help crashing into your caravan. I was trying to dodge that sheep." He pointed his thumb in the direction of the creature.

Wayne, or Visitor or whoever, gave all his attention to Tom's thumb, as if he couldn't guess what it was or what it might do.

Without taking his eyes off the stranger for a second, Tom backed over to the wreck of his bike and tugged it upright. The front wheel was almost folded in half.

"Aghhh! Look at that," Tom wailed.

"I surrender!" cried the blue boy, backing away, lifting his arms higher. He looked terrified. "No blastin', OK?" he begged.

"What are you on about?" Tom said, as soothingly as he could. The kid was obviously nuts. Tom gave his handlebars a gentle shake. "This is just my old bike. My BMX. See?"

"Your BMX-C?" echoed the stranger. "Is it loaded?"

"Loaded?" repeated Tom with a reassuring smile. "This isn't a weapon! It's a bike!"

"But it was in attack-mode, right?"

"It didn't smash into the tree on purpose, if that's what you mean," said Tom. "It was because of that sheep." He pointed back down the lane to where the sheep was quietly eating grass.

The blue boy looked startled. "Who's that? Is he with you?"

"The sheep? Don't be daft!" Suddenly Tom burst out laughing. "I know what this is," he said. "You're doing a stunt for charity, aren't you?"

Zeroed

It soon became quite clear that the blue boy had no idea what Tom was talking about. "Um, look, Wayne," he said kindly, trying to humour him, "there's no need to worry about me. Why don't you put your hands down and just tell me what you're doing here? I'm Tom, by the way." He glanced about him, saw where his football had rolled and ran to collect it.

"You're not goin' to blast me then?" asked Wayne, lowering his arms. He still seemed worried about the bike.

"Definitely not," said Tom. "I told you, this is just a bike. It's for going places fast – or it used to be." He side-footed the ball towards the stranger. It bobbled over the lumpy grass.

"Ah. A BMX-C's a transporter, then," said Wayne, looking relieved. "Noted. Beep." Without seeming even to look at the ball, he rolled it behind him and back-heeled it into the air. He ducked, caught the ball between his shoulder-blades, let it drop over his right shoulder and volleyed it against the trunk of the ash tree. It bounced straight back to him and he took it on his forehead, where it simply stuck for a second. Then with all the sting out of it, it dropped to his feet. He rested a shiny boot on it as gently as if it were an adoring puppy lying on its back waiting to have its tummy rubbed. "What about your friend over there?" he asked, nodding towards the lane.

"I told you, that's a sheep!" said Tom.

"Sheep," repeated Wayne. "Noted. Beep. So you're not the same species, yeah?"

"Sheep aren't human, if that's what you mean," said Tom, and it was at that moment that the penny dropped. "Flipping 'eck! I'm talking to an ALIEN!" he said to himself. He tried to keep calm and spoke as matter-of-factly as he could. "And you're not human either, are you?"

"I'm from a long way away," admitted Wayne.

"And you don't come from Manchester, do you?" said Tom.

"No. I come from Thought-Years away. From the planet Urd," explained Wayne. "I'm supposed to be collectin' useful information about planets in distant galaxies, yeah? Only thing is, I've had to make a bit of an emergency landin' here."

"Y-you mean this is a spaceship!" exclaimed Tom, taking a proper look at the "motor-home" for the first time.

"You might call him that," said the blue boy. "He's my Transporter. But the thing is, we've lost pressure in the Thought-Pump. If I can't fix the Thought-Pump before your planet spins 45 degrees, there's no way I can reset our positionin' co-ordinates. That means we've had it – me and my Transporter both. We shall never get home. We'll both lose power and get zeroed."

"Zeroed?" repeated Tom.

"Destroyed ... sucked into a

black hole."

"How long does it take for Earth to spin 45 degrees?" Tom asked, horrified, trying to do the maths. 360 degrees in 24 hours. So that's 360 divided by 24 …

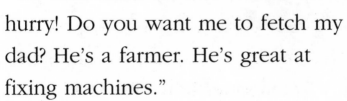

"You'd call it three hours."

"Wow. That's terrible!" said Tom. "We shall have to hurry! Do you want me to fetch my dad? He's a farmer. He's great at fixing machines."

"Your … dad? Farmer?"

"Um, he's my leader, sort of," Tom explained. "Well, he's my co-leader, with my mum. He lives at home on the farm. We can go and meet them if you like."

"Tom, mum, dad, farm. Noted," said Wayne. His eyes revolved very fast. He gave a satisfied little beep and puffs of vapour came out of his ears. Then he asked, "Will your dad have the right fixin'-material?"

"Good question!" said Tom. "I've no idea what you're going to need, but Dad keeps all sorts of useful stuff. It's worth asking."

"Then I'll disconnect the

Thought-Pump and bring him with me," Wayne said. He jumped astride the football, gripped it with his heels and looped it over his head into Tom's arms.

Wow! thought Tom.

Then Wayne dived under the spacecraft once again and came up carrying a glowing sphere, the size of a tennis ball. After that he spoke the words that every boy who likes a bit of excitement hopes to hear one day:

"Now take me to your leader."

A Ride On the Transporter

"We're gonna have to walk," said Tom, adding, "and I'm gonna have to carry the bike." With a grunt, he gathered the wreck of his BMX into his arms. "Can you carry the football?"

"Wait. Let me have a look at your transporter," said Wayne. "You take this." He passed the Thought-Pump to Tom. It was warm and soft as a chick. He slipped it into his pocket.

Wayne touched the bike. "How did he look before?"

Tom put the bike down and put his fists over his eyes as he tried to concentrate. It was going to be really hard to explain something as complicated as a bike to an alien.

"Thank you," said Wayne and when Tom opened his eyes he saw that Wayne had begun to shape the front wheel with his hands as if it were made of clay. "So this wheel goes like this and this bar ..." he gave it a twist, "... goes like this. Yeah?"

In a matter of seconds, there was Tom's BMX

looking as good as new!

"H-how on Earth …?" stammered Tom.

"The Thought-Pump's lost most of his power," explained Wayne. "But he can still do simple stuff – like readin' your mind, for instance. Once I got a look at your mind-picture, the rest was easy."

Tom started blushing. "Hey, I hope you're not looking into my mind all the time," he said. "Cos there's stuff in there I'd rather keep private."

"Don't worry, Tom," said Wayne. "I'll only look at stuff you want to share, yeah?"

"Oh," said Tom, relieved. "Well, thanks. And – er – seeing as you're in a hurry to get back home to Urd, it'll save a bit of time if we go two-up on the bike to find my dad." He patted the saddle. "Why don't you hop on while I pedal?"

Wayne looked mystified and then began jumping up and down on one leg.

"No, no!" said Tom. "Not that sort of hop! Wait! Sit like this." He sat astride the saddle to demonstrate.

Soon they were zooming two-up along back down the lane. The startled sheep left off chewing at the grass verge and crashed back into the field through another gap in the hedge.

"I get it; it's boy-powered!" shouted Wayne, hanging on to Tom's belt with one hand and holding the ball with the other. "And that sheep's brilliant. It's great the way he travels with his four corners in contact with the surface of the earth! Would you do us a favour and let us tune into your mind-picture again?"

"Be my guest," puffed Tom, wondering how an alien from the planet Urd could sound so much like a kid from Manchester.

Wayne instantly picked up what Tom was thinking. "I learned how to speak from the Thought-Pump," he answered. "His job is to pick up micro-waves from the atmosphere so that I can blend in with intelligent life-forces wherever we go. That's how come I found out that you like football and Wayne Rooney." He looked about him, excited by this amazing new world. "Hedge. Noted. Tree. Noted. Crow. Noted. Rabbit. Noted. Beep."

"So you're not actually Rooney, only Rooney the way I imagine him, is that it?"

"That's right," answered Wayne. "That, plus bits I picked up from hyperspace – off your internet, television, radio – stuff like that. There's information flying around everywhere in your atmosphere, see? So pickin' up virtual stuff is easy. But my mission is to report back with some real solid Earth Facts that I've tested for myself. This stuff you're showin' me is excellent! I only hope I can get it home."

"Well, you have made one little teeny mistake," said Tom aloud, trying not to hurt his passenger's feelings. "Rooney's not blue."

"Bloo? What's bloo?"

"The colour of your skin," Tom explained. "No humans are blue."

"Colour?" said Wayne, sounding worried. "I don't get you. We don't have colours on the dark side of the Moon of Treg!"

Tom knew exactly how it felt to have an impossible pile of homework and he suddenly felt really sorry for his poor lost passenger. "You'll be all right," he said. "I'll get you some useful Earth Facts and we'll see if Dad can fix your pump somehow, eh?"

Wayne Learns to Drive

By the time they reached the gate of Malt House Farm where Tom lived, he had started to get nervous about the way his mum and dad would react if he just turned up with a kid who was bright blue. "Um, let me get this right. You can blend in with intelligent life-forces, yes?"

"Yeah," said Wayne, "but ..."

"So you can change your shape to be anything that intelligent life-forms

34

want you to be. Right?"

"That's it … but …"

"So when we meet my mum and dad, could you look … just sort of quiet and polite?"

"Yeah, I can morph into anybody you like. But they might not be the right colour," warned Wayne.

"Wait here behind the shed while I fetch something," said Tom. "Keep out of sight till I get back." He dashed off.

"Shed," said Wayne. "Noted. Beep."

A minute later, Tom was back with his mother's make-up bag. He got cracking with the face-paint and the powder puff and it wasn't long before all Wayne's blue bits were looking a bit more normal – in a washed-out

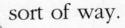

sort of way.

"Cool!" said Wayne. There was no sign of Tom's dad and the tractor was standing in the middle of the farmyard. "Oh, no! The Land Rover's gone," Tom told Wayne. "Dad's probably gone into town. Tell you what, we'll put the tractor away for him if you like and we'll have a nose round the workshop."

Wayne was staring at the tractor. Then he reached out and touched it. "He's warm," he said. "But I'm not gettin' any thought-waves off him."

Tom explained that this was just a machine, a vehicle used for working.

"Then how's he powered?" asked Wayne.

Tom struggled to explain what a diesel engine was and quickly gave up.

"I can't get what you're thinkin'," said Wayne, looking worried. "It's all a muddle. My Thought-Pump must be losing power fast!"

"Look. Best if I show you how it goes," said Tom. He jumped up into the seat and turned the key. As the engine roared into life, Wayne threw himself flat on the ground.

"It's all right! It won't hurt you!" called Tom, springing down and helping the terrified alien to get up. "It does exactly what you tell it. Look, I'll show you how it works.

Then we can put it away in the workshop. That's the barn over there; the building with the door open, next to the pig-sty."

"Pigs! Beautiful!" exclaimed Wayne. "Marvellous! Beep. Workshop. Beep. Barn. Door. Sty. Noted. Beep."

Tom sat him in the driver's seat and squatted down just behind him. He put his hands on Wayne's shoulders and closed his eyes while he concentrated. He thought hard about the way you use your hands and feet to drive; how you steer, shift gears, move forward and backward and stop.

Wayne didn't need telling twice. He revved the engine and went through the gears like a racing driver.

"Woah!" yelled Tom as the tractor whizzed round the yard. It shot through the gap between the buildings, out of the farm gate and into the lane. "Slow down!" screamed Tom.

Wayne seemed to be a little over-excited. "Practice!" he yelled and drove at top speed for five hundred metres until they reached the lower pasture. "Wheeee!"

Luckily the cows had been moved to the top meadow and the gate was open. Wayne spun the wheel, turned hard left and shot round the bumpy field four times, shouting. "Not smooth. Noted."

"You're not kidding!" wailed
Tom, feeling decidedly sea-sick.

"Beep. Barn. Back," muttered
Wayne while he calculated the
position of the workshop-barn. He
bent over the steering wheel, put
his shiny boot down and sent the
tractor roaring in that direction.
Chickens clucked and scattered and
pigs squealed as half a ton of tractor
ripped across the farmyard.

"We're gonna crash!" yelled Tom.
But somehow Wayne squeezed the
tractor through the open doors and
came to a shuddering halt in a cloud
of dust.

Tom unpeeled himself from the
back of the driver's seat and dropped

to the ground with his heart pounding.

"Ker-poom!" said Wayne, with a grin. "Ker-poom is good! Tract-or, eh? Hmm. He's slow, but well interestin'! Ker-poom! Noted. Beep."

"Thomas!" came a voice.

"Uh-oh, it's Dad," whispered Tom.

"Jethro"

Tom's dad was all muscle, a big-chested, tall man whose bulky overalls made him look even bigger. Tom did his best to look innocent. "Ah, you've put the tractor away for me. Thanks," said Mr Campbell cheerfully.

Phew. He'd missed the racing, then!

But as Mr Campbell's eyes got used to the dimness of the workshop, he realised that somebody else was standing beside him. "Jethro!" he said.

42

"Didn't see you there for a moment. What can I do for you, my friend?"

Tom gave a start. Jethro? Jethro Burgess was a small-holder from just over the hill who always wore the same raggy old pullover. He was an old mate of his dad's, a great tub of a bloke with a big, sunburnt bald head, and always popping in for a chat. Whenever he met Tom, he had a habit of covering the boy's head with one huge rough hand.

Suddenly Tom felt his skull getting a squeeze like a melon. He was here! But how on earth did he …? The penny dropped. It was Wayne!

Somehow he'd puffed himself up like a balloon and morphed into their neighbour.

"As oi wuz jest saying to Tommy-boy here," came a voice almost exactly like Jethro's only more on one note, "the case on this here pump is leaking. Oi don't s'pose you've got a bit of jollop that'll seal him?"

Mr Campbell cocked his ear as he always did when Jethro started jabbering and stooped to look at the Thought-Pump. The glow of it was fading a bit, but it still gave off some light. "Well I'm darned if I've seen anything like this!" he said, turning it in his fingers.

"Sealed unit," said Wayne-Jethro, grabbing it back. "D'you mind if oi have a bit of a rummage on your work-bench? Oi need to fix it in a hurry, see?"

"Help yourself," said Mr Campbell, scratching his head. "Jethro" dipped his fingers into some paint and gave them a lick.

"Nope." He sucked at the neck of an oil-can. "Nope." He grabbed a can of WD-40 and squirted some up his nostril. "Nope." A bottle of turpentine? Slurp. "Nope!" He was getting more and more frantic. "None o' these is any use. Oo-eck! Looks loik oi'm zeroed, then."

"What d'you mean, 'zeroed'?" asked Mr Campbell. "You feeling all right, Jethro, old boy?"

"Er … Jest a bit fuddled," came the answer.

"Thomas, take Jethro into the house and ask Mum to put the kettle on. Meanwhile, I'll have a look and see if I can lay my hands on something that might do as a sealant. Go ahead. I'll join you in a tick."

Crunching Cakes

As Tom and Wayne stepped into the warm kitchen, Tom's mum had her back to them and was turning out a fruit cake on to a plate.

"Trust you to smell cake, Thomas," she said with a laugh. Then she noticed his companion. "Oh, hello, Bertie!" she said, tidying up her hair. "Haven't seen you for ages! How are you? Gosh, you haven't been over-doing it, have you? You're looking rather pale."

Bertie? thought Tom. And then he twigged that Wayne had morphed into Albert Kensington, the swottiest kid in his class.

"Yes, well, I came to pick Tom's brain, Mrs Campbell," said Wayne-Bertie. "He's highly intelligent, you know."

"Really?" said Tom's mum, going all pink and pleased. "Will you have a slice of cake, Bertie?"

"Cake? Beep. Noted. Smashing!" said Wayne-Bertie. "Would you mind telling me precisely how it's constructed?"

"Well, um, I can tell you the ingredients, if that's what you mean," said Mrs Campbell. She reached for her cookbook and began to rattle them off.

Wayne noted them, and as he did so, lifted the plate with his slice of cake on it and took a huge bite out of both.

Tom's eyes nearly popped out. "Er ... can we have some of this plum jam on top, Mum?" he said loudly, trying to drown the sound of Wayne crunching china. He reached for one of the newly filled jam-jars next to the stove.

Mum stopped reading out the list of ingredients and shouted, "Wait!"

Uh-oh! Now we're for it! thought Tom.

But Mum went on, "That's far too hot! Let me get you some I made yesterday. Here." She bent down and took a jar out of a cupboard – which gave Tom time to try to send a thought-message about not eating plates.

A moment later, Mum was spreading generous spoonfuls of rich, red, sticky sweetness over the top of the remains of her cake with the words "It's nice and thick. I put extra pectin in it. Would you like another slice, Bertie?"

Wayne-Bertie leaned over and gave the jam on her cake a good lick with a long blue tongue.

"Bertie!" cried Mum. "That's disgusting! How dare you!"

"Eureka!" yelled Wayne. "Let's go, Tom!"

With that, he stuffed the rest of his slice, plate and all, into his mouth, grabbed Tom by the scruff of the neck and hoisted him out of the door.

Mates

Well, there's one good thing, thought Tom as he pedalled Wayne two-up back down the lane towards the common. At least Mum won't be inviting Bertie to tea in a hurry.

He heard a humming behind him. "He's workin' again – my Thought-Pump!" cried Wayne. "That jam was just the job! It was the pectin in it!"

"How come?" puffed Tom.

"Hetero-polysaccharide," said Wayne.

"What?"

"It's a type of carbohydrate," explained Wayne. "You get it on Urd, but I never realised you have it here on Earth, too! If you heat it to about 108 degrees centigrade, the molecules tangle together in a chain made up of galacturonic sugar acid units! Amazin'!"

"I see," said Tom, although to be honest, he didn't have a clue what Wayne was on about. By now they were back at the spacecraft and Wayne dived underneath it to re-connect the Thought-Pump. As he re-appeared, Tom said, rather sadly, "You'll be off now, I s'pose."

"Yeah, well …"

"That's a shame, because I was

really hoping to introduce you to my mates ..." He didn't speak the rest of what was on his mind. "Mate," said Wayne, thoughtfully. "You're my mate. Right?"

"That's right."

"You wait till I tell 'em back home! That's really special, that is!" Wayne glanced up at the sun and grinned back at Tom. "Well, look, there's a few more degrees for the earth to rotate before Zero-Hour, so I can't see any harm in doing what you want me to," he said. "Besides, I owe you one, because you've given me some brilliant Earth Facts to take back to Urd with me."

"Like what?" asked Tom.

"Like pigs for a start. Beautiful! And mum and dad and barns. And your transporters – BMX-Cs and tractors. And sheep and rabbits and crows. Then there's hedges and trees. And more important than that lot, there's cake and colours and plum jam. Not to mention mates and football. Wow, it's been great findin' out what a mate is! And do you know what? I'd love to try a kick-about before I take off."

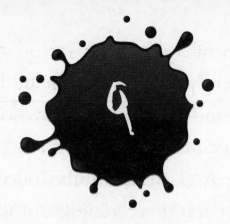

The Goal No One Will Forget

And so it was that Tom came to be hiding in the long grass in the shadow of the old cricket pavilion on Spearmarsh Common, watching himself – or rather, somebody who looked and sounded very much like him – challenge his footballing mates over on the practice-pitch.

"Woo! Where'd you get them fancy boots from, Tom?" somebody yelled. Ah, so Wayne had decided to keep his own footwear on, then.

"Yeah, you may laugh!" he heard Wayne say to Peter as the whole crowd of boys gathered round. "But I'm prepared to take on the lot of you."

"Oh, you're prepared, are you, Tommo?" said Harvey.

"Prepared to get murdered, more like!" put in Kyle with a hoot of laughter.

"First to five," said Wayne, putting his head on one side just as Tom did when he got serious.

"Then I've got to be … well, somewhere else."

"Look, I'll go with Tom, give him a bit of a chance," said Ned, stepping up alongside Wayne. Good old Ned. He didn't want Tom to make too much of a fool of himself.

"No, you're all right," said Wayne. "That's nice of you. But no thanks – I want to take on the lot of you together if you don't mind. All right with everyone if I kick off?"

"Ready when you are," called Dom, jogging back to take up his usual defensive position in front of Logie.

And kick off Wayne did.

He moved so fast, he seemed hardly to touch the grass as he

zigzagged among the screaming
opposition players, yet when
anybody tried to get a tackle, he
could stop and turn in a split second.
He jigged his way past the whole
lot of them and walked the ball over
the goal-line before toe-poking it up
to shake the net.

"Hoy! Not fair! We weren't ready!"
moaned Logie, bending to pick the
ball up.

"Sorry. Thought you were,"
said the Tom look-
alike. "Why don't
you lot kick off
this time?"
This time the home
side decided to
play keep-ball,

spreading out and slipping passes back and forth while "Tom" skipped from side to side, watching and waiting. If anyone had taken a moment to look at the eyes that followed the ball, they would have seen them revolving like miniature blue planets.

Nobody expected him to get back in time to defend his goal but "Tom" was suddenly there, right in the middle of it. He kicked up his leg and smothered Harvey's cracking shot with a cushioned side-foot so that it dropped stone-dead just in front of him.

While Harvey stood stunned, "Tom" slipped the ball through his open legs, and was away! He didn't hurry. He let the players come at him in turn and – just when they thought they had the ball – he would slip them a dummy and roll it away under his boot.

The fifth goal was something neither Tom nor his mates would ever forget.

Wayne was on the halfway line when lanky Gabby slid it, throwing himself full length to capture the ball. It was a dangerous tackle, even though no studs were involved. It could have done real damage to the

ankle of any normal kid. "Tom"
wasn't bothered one bit. He gave
the ball a little dink over the flying
legs and let Gabby crash past like a
thundering bull. There were now six
players between the kid on the ball
and the goal.

If there was any back-swing,
nobody saw it, but suddenly, in one
flowing move, "Tom" lifted the ball
knee-level and volleyed it – Ker-poom!
– over the heads of the lot of them.

Logie made one of his famous

death-
defying
leaps but the
ball curled
away from
his flapping

hand and flew right into the top corner of the goal.

"Blimey!"

"Wha … at?"

"Wow!"

"Fluke!"

"Where did THAT come from?"

Wayne couldn't resist it. "It came from outer space!" he yelled as he punched the air.

He pulled his T-shirt over his head and danced his way off the pitch until he disappeared from sight.

The real Tom took the opportunity to creep away. "He's gone," he thought sadly.

Well, however rubbish he was at football in future, at least his mates would never be able to forget how he'd run rings round the lot of them on this amazing afternoon.

But what about that celebration! Taking his shirt off and waving it about was one thing. But they'd never know why it looked like Tom had painted himself blue all over ...